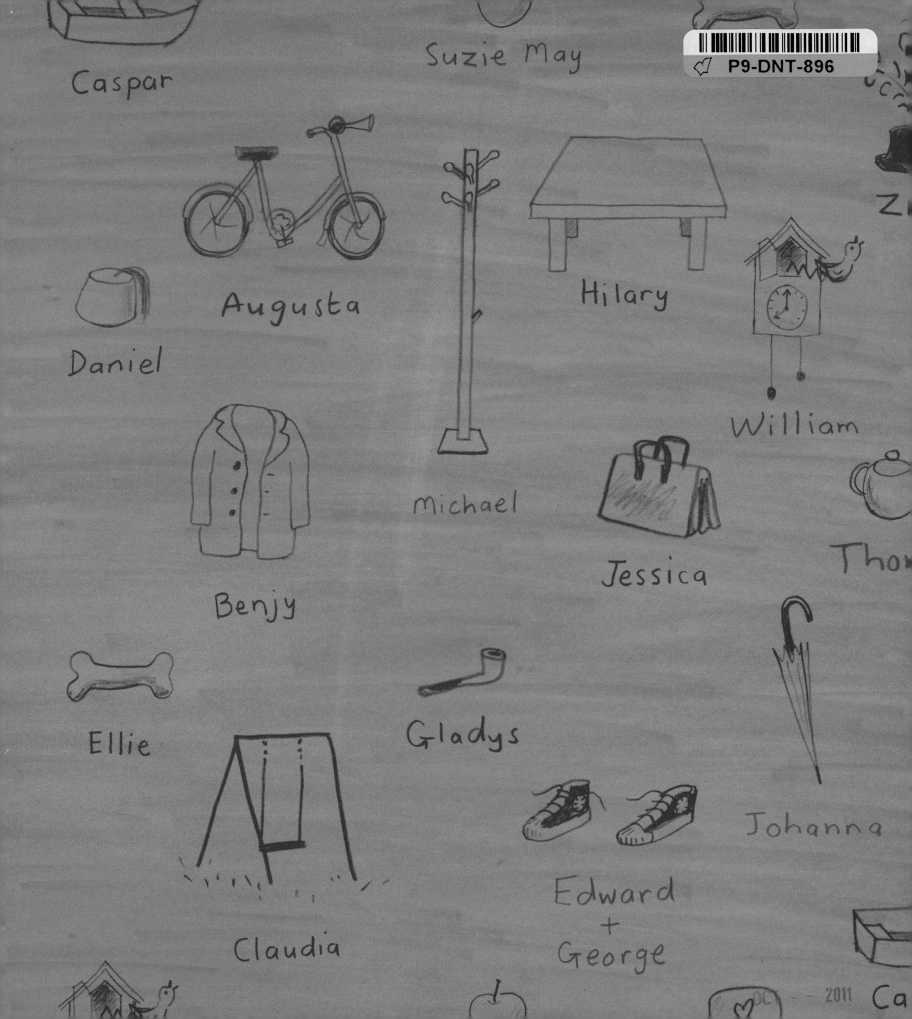

Caspar

Suzie May

Augusta

Hilary

Z

Daniel

William

Benjy

michael

Jessica

Tho

Ellie

Gladys

Johanna

Claudia

Edward
+
George

2011

Once there was a pencil, a lonely little pencil, and nothing else.
It lay there, which was nowhere in particular, for a long, long time.
Then one day that little pencil made a move, shivered slightly,
quivered somewhat . . . and began to draw.

First U.S. edition 2008

Library of Congress Cataloging-in-Publication Data
is available.

Library of Congress Catalog Card Number 2007051885

ISBN 978-0-7636-3894-8

10 9 8 7 6 5

Printed in Singapore

This book was typeset in Gill Sans MT SchoolBook.
The illustrations were done in acrylic.

Candlewick Press
99 Dover Street
Somerville, Massachusetts 02144

visit us at www.candlewick.com

Pencil

CANDLEWICK PRESS

# Allan Ahlberg • Bruce Ingman

The pencil drew a boy.

"What's my name?" said the boy.

"Er . . . Banjo," said the pencil.

"Good," said Banjo. "Draw me a dog."

The pencil drew a dog.

"What's my name?" barked the dog.

"Er . . . Bruce," said the pencil.

"Excellent," said Bruce. "Draw me a cat."

The pencil hesitated.

"Please!" said Bruce.

So then the pencil drew a cat (named Mildred),
and Bruce, of course, chased Mildred . . .

and Banjo chased Bruce,

'round and 'round the house, which the pencil drew,
up and down the road, which the pencil drew,
and in and out of the park, which the pencil drew.

They ran around for a long, long time,
getting hot and bothered, tired and grumpy . . .
and hungry.

"Draw me an apple," said Banjo.

"Draw me a bone," barked Bruce.

"Draw me a . . . mouse?" meowed Mildred.

"No," said the pencil. "No mouse."

"All right, cat food, then," meowed Mildred.

Only then,
"We can't eat this . . ."
"Apple!" yelled Banjo.
"Bone!" barked Bruce.
"Cat food!" meowed Mildred.

# "IT'S BLACK AND WHITE!"

The pencil hesitated, frowned,
looked thoughtful for a while, and drew . . .

# A PAINTBRUSH.

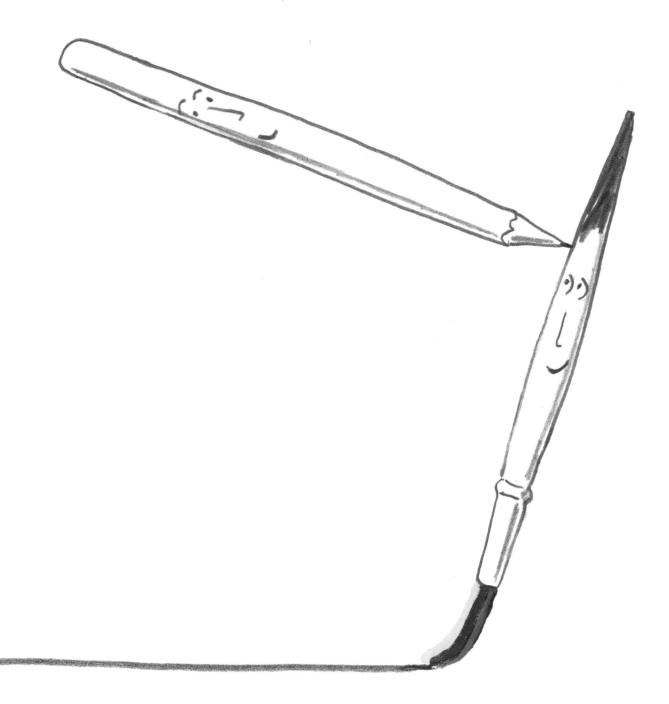

"What's my name?" said the paintbrush.
"Er . . . Kitty," said the pencil.
"Splendid," said Kitty. "How can I help?"

After that, Kitty painted the apple and the bone and the cat food.
She painted Banjo and Bruce, but not Mildred.
Mildred was a black-and-white cat, anyway.
She painted the house and the road and the park.

"What next?" cried the now cheerful and excited pencil.
"Anything!" yelled Kitty. She was excited, too.
"You draw and I'll color it!"

So they did.

Banjo got a little sister, named Elsie,
and a mom and dad, named Mr. and Mrs.,
some grandmas and grandpas,
three or four cousins, and an Uncle Charlie.
Bruce got a friend—an Airedale named Polly—
and a ball.

"What's my name?" said the ball.

"Don't be silly," said the pencil.

 The ball made a sad face.

"All right, then . . . Sebastian," said the pencil.

Then, all of a sudden—TROUBLE.
Banjo kicked Sebastian—"Oh!"—
into the air and broke a window.
Polly ran off with Bruce's bone.
"What's my name?" said the bone.
One of Mildred's kittens—
which she had just asked for—
got stuck up a tree.
And EVERYBODY was grumpy
and starting to complain.

"This hat looks silly," said Mrs.
"My ears are too big," said Mr.
"I shouldn't be *smoking a pipe*," said a grandpa.
"Get rid of these ridiculous sneakers!" yelled Elsie.

The pencil hesitated, frowned,
looked worried for a while, quivered somewhat,
and drew . . .

# AN ERASER.

After that, the eraser,
as you might expect,
rubbed things out—
hats and ears and such.
The pencil and the paintbrush
drew and painted them again.
Everybody was HAPPY.

Only then—MORE TROUBLE.
The eraser rubbed other things out.
(He was excited, too.)

He rubbed the table out
and the chair out
and the rug out,

and the front door out,                    and the house out.

He rubbed the tree out
and the kitten (who was still up it) out
and the other kittens out.
And the cousins
and the grandmas
and Uncle Charlie—

# OUT! OUT! OUT!

He rubbed the road out
and the park out
and the sky out.
He rubbed everything—
even Kitty the paintbrush—
OUT!

Now, once more, there was only the pencil,
that lonely little pencil, and nothing else.

The eraser kept on coming.
The pencil drew a wall to stop him.
The eraser rubbed it out.

He drew a cage to keep him in.
The eraser rubbed it out.

He drew a river and some mountains, with
lions and tigers and bears—"Oh, my!"
The eraser rubbed them out.

Then, when all seemed lost and there was absolutely no escape,
that brave and clever little pencil quivered somewhat,
shivered slightly, and drew . . .

# ANOTHER ERASER.

And what did these TWO ERASERS do?
(Their names were Ronald and Rodney, by the way.)
Yes, of course, as you will surely guess,
they rubbed each other . . .

OUT!

After that—of course, of course!—the pencil drew
Banjo and Bruce, Mildred and the others all over again,
and Kitty—he drew her as well—colored them in.

He put the sun back in the sky,
the house back on the road,
the kitten back up the tree,
the grass back in the park,
and a *picnic*—a lovely brand-new picnic—out on the grass.

The picnic lasted for a long, long time.
Banjo played soccer with Sebastian—"Oh!"—and his little cousins.
Banjo's dad tried eating a boiled egg, named Billy, but it ran off.
A whole column of ants ("What're *our* names?" said the ants.*)
came marching across the picnic cloth.

*Alice,    Alvie,    Abraham,    Amy,    Araminta,    Alberic,    Algernon,    Anastasia,    Ada,    and    Allan.

Finally the sun went down,
the eating and the games and the adventures
stopped, and everybody—and everything—
went home to bed.

The pencil drew a moon in the sky
and some darkening hills.
And Kitty the paintbrush painted them.
He drew a snug little box with a cozy lining.
And Kitty painted that.

She painted him, too.